This title was originally catalogued by the Library of Congress as follows: Seuss, Dr. Dr. Seuss's ABC. New York, Beginner Books, 1963. 63 p. col. illus. 24 cm. "B-30." I. Title. Dr. Seuss, pseud. of Theodor Seuss Geisel. PZ8.3.G276Dm 63-17261 ISBN 0-394-80030-3 ISBN 0-394-90030-8 (lib. bdg.)

# Dr. Seuss's ABC

Beginner Books

# BIG A

little      a

What begins with A?

Aunt Annie's alligator .

..... A ... a ... A

# BIG B

little        b

# What begins with B?

Barber
baby
bubbles
and a
bumblebee.

# BIG C

little       c

What begins with C?

Camel on the ceiling
C . . . . c . . . . C

# BIG D

## little d

David Donald Doo
dreamed
a dozen doughnuts
and
a duck-dog, too.

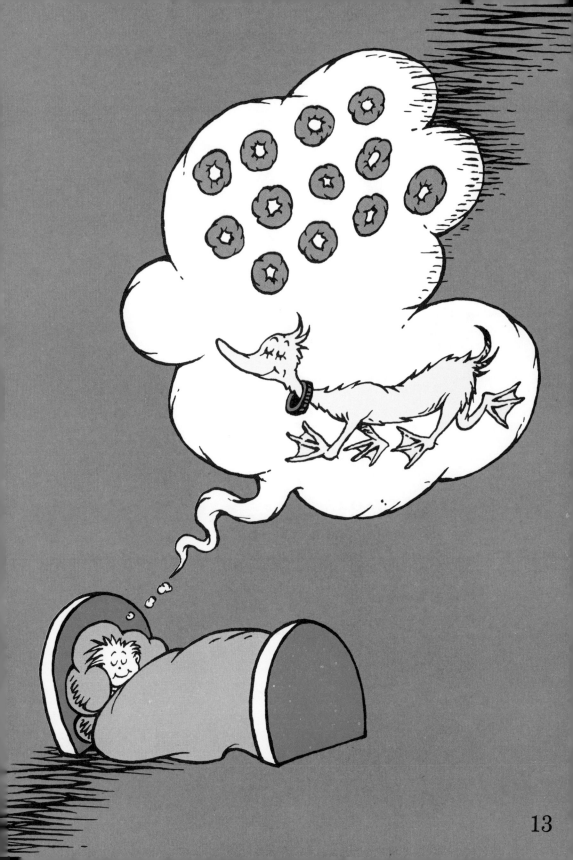

# ABCDE..e..e

ear

egg

elephant

e

e

E

# BIG F

little       f

F .. f .. F

Four fluffy feathers
on a
Fiffer-feffer-feff.

17

# ABCD
# EFG

Goat
girl
googoo goggles
G . . . g . . . G

# BIG H

little      h

Hungry horse.
Hay.

Hen in a hat.
Hooray !
Hooray !

# BIG I

little        i

i . . . . i . . . . i

Icabod
is
itchy.

So am I.

# BIG J

little            j

What begins with j?

Jerry Jordan's
jelly jar
and jam
begin that way.

# BIG K

little       k

Kitten. Kangaroo.

Kick a kettle.
Kite
and a
king's kerchoo.

# BIG L

little        l

Little Lola Lopp.
Left leg.
Lazy lion
licks a lollipop.

29

# BIG M

little           m

Many mumbling mice
are making
midnight music
in the moonlight . . .

mighty nice

31

# BIG N

little         n

What begins with those?

Nine new neckties
and a nightshirt
and a nose.

O is very useful.
You use it when you say:
"Oscar's only ostrich
oiled
an orange owl today."

ABCD
EFG
HIJK
LMNO...

...P

Painting pink pajamas.
Policeman in a pail.

Peter Pepper's puppy.
And now
Papa's in the pail.

# BIG Q
little      q

What begins with Q ?

The quick
Queen of Quincy
and her
quacking quacker-oo.

QUACK

QUACK

41

# BIG R
### little r

Rosy Robin Ross.

Rosy's going riding
on her
red rhinoceros.

# BIG S

little      s

Silly Sammy Slick
sipped six sodas
and got
sick sick sick.

# T . . . . . T
### t . . . . . . . t

## What begins with T?

## Ten tired turtles
## on a tuttle-tuttle tree.

47

# BIG U

little        u

What begins with U?

Uncle Ubb's umbrella
and his
underwear, too.

# BIG V

little     v

Vera Violet Vinn
 is
very
very
very awful
on her violin.

W .. w .. W

Willy Waterloo
washes Warren Wiggins
who is
washing Waldo Woo.

**X** is very useful
if your name is
Nixie Knox.
It also
comes in handy
spelling ax
and extra fox.

NIXIE KNOX

# BIG Y

little   y

A yawning yellow yak.
Young Yolanda Yorgenson
is yelling on his back.

QRS
TUV...

W..X
Y.. and ....

# BIG Z

little            z

## What begins with Z?

I do.

I am a
Zizzer-Zazzer-Zuzz
as you can
plainly see.